# Bizzy Mizz Lizzie

## DAVID SHANNON

THE BLUE SKY PRESS

An Imprint of Scholastic Inc. • New York

FOR BIZZY MIZZ EMMA AND HER AMAZING MOM

THE BLUE SKY PRESS

Library of Congress catalog card number: 2016041994

ISBN 978-0-545-61943-1

10 9 8 7 6 5 4 3 2 1        17 18 19 20 21

Printed in the U.S.A.        88        First edition, October 2017

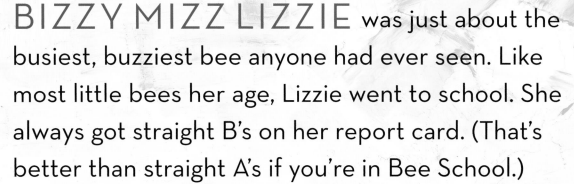

BIZZY MIZZ LIZZIE was just about the busiest, buzziest bee anyone had ever seen. Like most little bees her age, Lizzie went to school. She always got straight B's on her report card. (That's better than straight A's if you're in Bee School.)

Lizzie did lots of things besides school, too.

She took dance lessons, acting lessons, art lessons, and music lessons.

She also played Bee League baseball,

and she was a member of the Junior Honey Scouts.

Everyone asked, "Why so busy, Mizz Lizzie?"

"Because someday I want to meet the Queen," Lizzie answered. "And when she asks me if I'm the best bee I can be, I'll say, 'Yes, ma'am, I am!'"

Of course, Lizzie had lots of friends.

Bizzy Mizz Lizzie's best friend was Lazy Mizz Daizy. Daizy was just the opposite of Lizzie. She liked to go to the Garden and lie down in a big flower. "It smells wonderful!" she told Lizzie. "Do you want to come with me?"

"I'm too busy for that," Lizzie always said.

Lizzie's other friends were quite busy and buzzy, though. Some of them did *some* things with her. Others did *other* things with her.

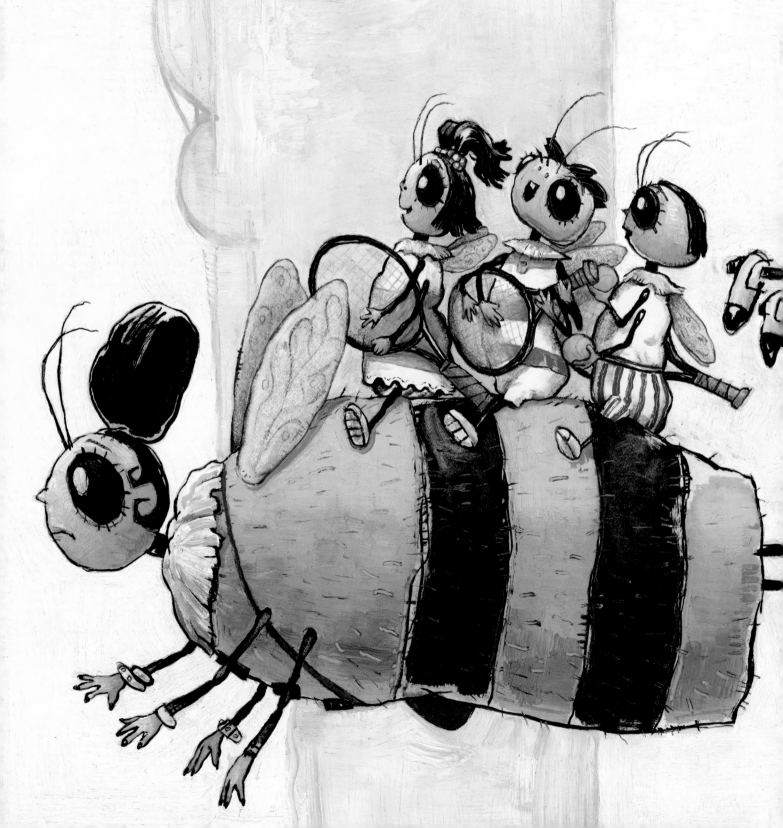

But Bizzy Mizz Lizzie did *everything*!

The only bee that was maybe even busier than Lizzie was her mom.

One day, everyone in Hivetown was buzzing with some exciting news. There was going to be a big Spelling Contest!

The busiest, buzziest little bees were going to compete, and the winner would get to meet the Queen!

The three lucky bees chosen for the contest were:
Newzy Suzie, who knew pretty much everything about
everything. Zach Zack Pat-on-the-Back, who never,
*ever* got in trouble, and . . . BIZZY MIZZ LIZZIE!

Lizzie was so thrilled she just about buzzed herself silly. "This is my big chance!" she shouted.

Lizzie studied so hard for the Spelling Contest that she barely got any sleep.

"I'm worried about you," said her mom. "You need to rest."

Daizy agreed. "Why don't you take a day off and go to the Garden with me?"

Lizzie was cranky. "I don't see how you can just lie around and do nothing!" she said.

"Well, I like doing nothing," Daizy replied. "It's nice to just think about things. And sometimes I read a book, or I talk to other bees. Last time, I met a very nice old lady who knows lots of stories. You should meet her."

"I'm too busy," said Lizzie, again. "Tomorrow is the Big Day!"

Daizy smiled. "Lizzie, you're the most amazing bee I know. I'm sure you'll win."

"If I can stay awake!" joked Lizzie.

The next day, the entire colony was at the Spelling Contest. Everyone buzzed as loud as they could when the Queen arrived. Newzy Suzie, Zach Zack Pat-on-the-Back, and Lizzie battled through round after round. But then Suzie forgot a "z" in "razzmatazz," and Zach Zack was fooled by "bamboozle." All Lizzie had to do was spell "quizzical" and she would win! She closed her eyes to think.

And then it happened. . . .

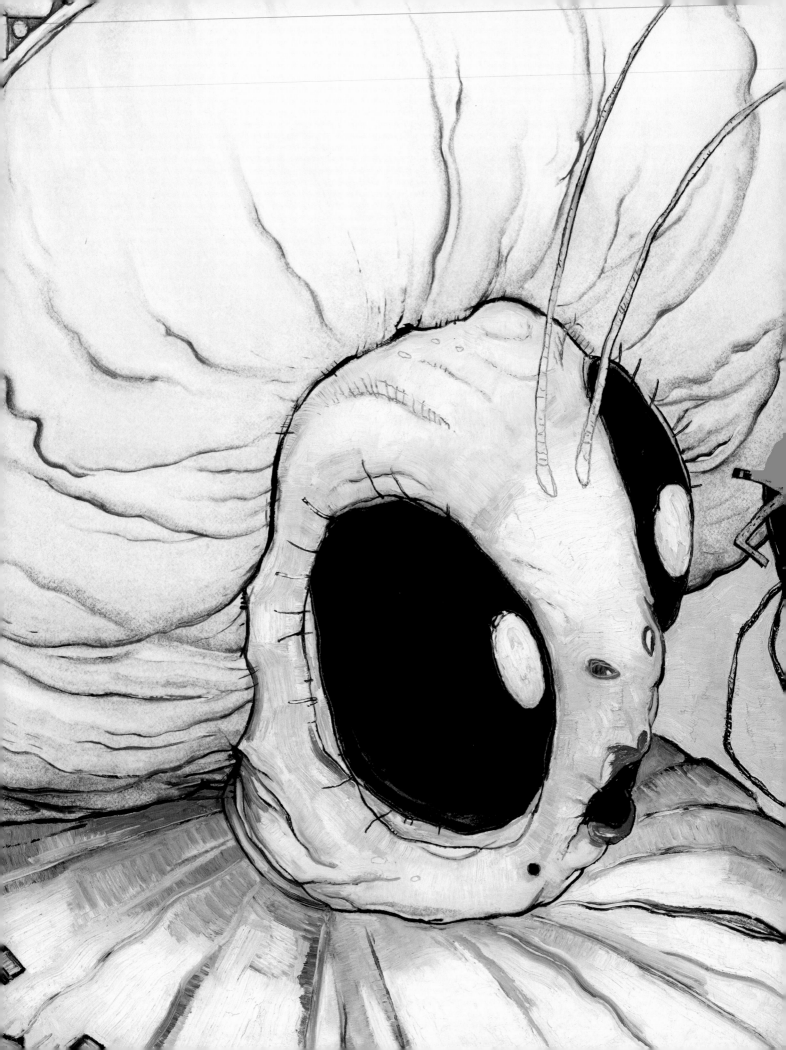

Bizzy Mizz Lizzie dozed off.

She woke up shouting, "Q-U-I-Z-Z-I-C-A-L!" Her mom
and Daizy were next to her bed. "I have to get back to
the contest!" Lizzie cried. "I have to meet the Queen!"

"That was three days ago," said Lizzie's mom. "The
doctor says nothing but rest for you now. I'm so sorry.
I should have said that a long time ago."

"Well," said Lizzie, trying not to cry, "at least
now I can go to the Garden with Daizy."

"Good idea," said Lizzie's mom.

"It's so beautiful!" Lizzie gasped as they lay back in a flower. But she was still thinking about the contest. "Maybe I should go home and study my spelling, though—for next year."

"Who thinks about spelling in the middle of a garden?!" said a strange voice.

Lizzie looked up and saw an old bee smiling at her.

Daizy shouted, "That's my friend I told you about!"

Lizzie thought the old bee looked familiar. Then she realized. . . . "Y-you're the Queen!" she exclaimed.

"You are?" mumbled Daizy. "What happened to your big hair?"

The Queen laughed. "Oh, I wear my wig so they have something to put that silly crown on!"

"But aren't you too busy to be here?" Lizzie asked.

"I'm busy doing *nothing*," answered the Queen. "It helps me be the best bee I can be."

Lizzie knew exactly what the Queen meant. "If I wasn't so tired, I would have won the Spelling Contest. . . ." She sighed.

"Yup," said the Queen. "But then you probably wouldn't be here. And aren't you happy right now?"

Lizzie thought for a second. There she was in the beautiful Garden with her best friend . . . and *the Queen!* "Yes, ma'am, I am!" she replied.

And that's how Bizzy Mizz Lizzie learned to stop and smell the flowers, which, when you think about it, is exactly what bees are supposed to do.